The Whodamagoodafoodawhoda

Written by **T. K. GIGLER**

Illustrated by **CLANCY BUNDY**

Fulton Books, Inc.
Meadville, PA

Published by Fulton Books 2020

ISBN 978-1-64654-757-9 (paperback)
ISBN 978-1-64654-758-6 (digital)

Printed in the United States of America

To my daughter Shannon

As the sun rose above Sugar Cone Mountain, the Fooderites began to stir.

The village was buzzing with excitement. It was the day of the "Whodamagoodafoodawhoda Festival."

For the citizens of Fooderland, it was the greatest holiday of the year.

You see, there was only one Whoodamagoodafoodawhoda to be found each year.

And every third day of the third month, it would appear to one lucky child.

It was said that the special treat was the sweetest, yummiest pastry in all the land.

But the best part of the day was if you were lucky enough and had a good heart, you had a chance to find the Whodamagoodafoodawhoda.

Then with the last bite, you were granted one wish.

But the wish had to be pure of heart! A selfish wish would not be granted. Although because the

Whodamagoodafoodawhoda was so difficult to find, it was thought it only appeared to the worthy.

The only Fooderites allowed to compete were the children. They had to be between the ages of eight and twelve. This way, the winners were thought to have the innocence required.

The festivities were overseen by the king and queen of Fooderland. They were loved and admired throughout the land. The king was a rather plump man. When he was a child, he was lucky enough to find and eat a Whodamagoodafoodawhoda! And his wish, of course, was to be king. And a wonderful king he became. But as we

all know, the pastry was quite delicious, and ever since, he maintained a fondness for yummy baked treats. This not only made him rather large but extremely happy.

As the festivities were about to begin, the children participating were being prepared by their parents.

Other than words of encouragement, there wasn't anything they could tell their children—at least nothing that would help.

It was going to be a glorious day!

The Fooderites, like any other people, had opinions on which child had the best chance to find the Whodamagoodafoodawhoda. It added to the excitement of the day.

It was time! There were four eligible children this year. There was Edward, the baker's son.

Clayton was the son of the schoolteacher. He was thought to be the front runner.

And lastly, there were the twins, Emma and Kaylie! They never took anything too seriously.

The quest would begin as soon as the sun's rays hit the starting line.

And as the light crept toward the line, the crowd became electric.

As it lit up, they were off. For the first hundred yards, there was only one path…

Beyond, there were four main paths that would split into four more. Nobody knew which path to take, nor did anyone really know what to look for.

Clayton was the first to decide. He headed east.

The twins took off to the far west, determined to outwit the teacher's son. Edward could hear them begin to sing as they skipped away. With two paths left to choose from, he chose and trekked on.

Nobody knew exactly what the tree looked like. As a matter of fact, only legend told them that the Whodamagoodafoodawhoda grows on a tree.

Previous winners could not remember once they ate the pastry, which deepened the mystery. This made the challenge much more difficult.

Clayton had walked for almost an hour when he saw his first tree. Now there was a great variety of bushes and flowers in Fooderland, but trees were rare. He had kept on his chosen path and would stick to it.

His mother had always said, "It's when you change your mind that you make the wrong choice. Your first thought is usually the correct one."

As he came up to the tree, he saw no blooms. So seeing no other choice, he hid, waited, and watched.

On the other side of the mountain, the twins were still skipping and singing down their chosen path. They believed if they acted innocent and carefree, they would find the prize. Suddenly, they came upon a tree. This tree was full of blooms.

The girls jumped into the tree, searching for the elusive pastry.

They also found nothing. So like Clayton, they waited and watched. The difference being, they played at the trunk of the tree, singing and laughing while hoping for the best.

Edward was beginning to tire. His heart was not in the challenge. He worried about his father, the baker.

His father's goods could not live up to the legend of the Whodamagoodafoodawhoda, at least that is what he believed.

The fact was, he was just unhappy. Edward's father had told him that if he finds the pastry, bring it back to him, so he may make one himself. Edward knew this was wrong, so his efforts were less than the others.

His father's happiness was all that mattered. As all the others waited for their trees to bloom a pastry, Edward sat down and rested. No sign of any trees! He put his head in his hands and began to cry.

Suddenly, he heard a rumbling sound.

The ground beneath him began to shake. As he looked up, his mouth dropped wide open!

Before his eyes, out of nowhere, a sprout began to emerge next to his feet.

He quickly backed away.

It was growing at an unbelievable rate. And in what seemed like an instant, it was a full-grown tree.

And yes, it had bloomed a perfect Whodamagoodafoodawhoda!

Edward wiped the tears from his eyes and gently picked
the pastry from the tree.

At that moment, Edward thought of his father. If he did what his father asked, it would make him very happy. He loved his father! Pondering all, he headed down the mountain with his prize.

As he approached the end of his journey, he could see the crowd, including his father, cheering him on. When he reached the finish line, his father stepped toward him.

Edward looked at his father still in tears and shoved the Whodamagoodafoodawhoda into his mouth.

"Wow!" the crowd yelled.

His father dropped his head.

And as quickly as the cheering began, it stopped. Now Edward was to make his wish. As he swallowed the last mouthful, he cleared his throat and paused.

Edward only wanted one thing. "I want my father to be filled with happiness forever!"

The crowd cheered and a feeling of pride was shared by all.

There were many things he could have wished for, but Edward never wanted for himself.

He only cared about others. His father's happiness returned, and his business began to thrive.

Some say the child finds the Whodamagoodafoodawhoda,
but I think we all know, it's the other way around.

About the Author

T. K. Gigler was born and raised in Spokane, Washington. He is married with one daughter and three grandchildren. He attended Gonzaga University where he received a BA in liberal arts. His grandchildren are his inspiration.

CPSIA information can be obtained
at www.ICGtesting.com
Printed in the USA
LVHW071359071020
668196LV00022B/1471

9 781646 547579